W9-BIV-098

E
BOE

Boelts, Maribeth,
1964-

Dogerella.

$11.99   06/19/2008

DATE			

BAKER & TAYLOR

Dear Parent:

Congratulations! Your child is taking the first steps on an exciting journey. The destination? Independent reading!

STEP INTO READING® will help your child get there. The program offers five steps to reading success. Each step includes fun stories and colorful art. There are also Step into Reading Sticker Books, Step into Reading Math Readers, Step into Reading Write-In Readers, Step into Reading Phonics Readers, and Step into Reading Phonics First Steps! Boxed Sets—a complete literacy program with something for every child.

Learning to Read, Step by Step!

Ready to Read   Preschool–Kindergarten
• big type and easy words • rhyme and rhythm • picture clues
For children who know the alphabet and are eager to begin reading.

Reading with Help   Preschool–Grade 1
• basic vocabulary • short sentences • simple stories
For children who recognize familiar words and sound out new words with help.

Reading on Your Own   Grades 1–3
• engaging characters • easy-to-follow plots • popular topics
For children who are ready to read on their own.

Reading Paragraphs   Grades 2–3
• challenging vocabulary • short paragraphs • exciting stories
For newly independent readers who read simple sentences with confidence.

Ready for Chapters   Grades 2–4
• chapters • longer paragraphs • full-color art
For children who want to take the plunge into chapter books but still like colorful pictures.

STEP INTO READING® is designed to give every child a successful reading experience. The grade levels are only guides. Children can progress through the steps at their own speed, developing confidence in their reading, no matter what their grade.

Remember, a lifetime love of reading starts with a single step!

To my dog-loving niece, Ayoko —M.B.

To Vince —D.W.

Text copyright © 2008 by Maribeth Boelts
Illustrations copyright © 2008 by Donald Wu

All rights reserved.
Published in the United States by Random House Children's Books, a division of Random House, Inc., New York.

Step Into Reading, Random House, and the Random House colophon are registered trademarks of Random House, Inc.

www.stepintoreading.com

Educators and librarians, for a variety of teaching tools, visit us at www.randomhouse.com/teachers

Library of Congress Cataloging-in-Publication Data
Boelts, Maribeth.
Dogerella / by Maribeth Boelts ; illustrated by Donald Wu. — 1st ed.
    p. cm. (Step into reading. Step 3)
Summary: With the help of her fairy dogmother, Dogerella gets the chance to attend Princess Bea's ball where the princess will select the best dog to be her royal pet.
ISBN 978-0-375-83393-9 (trade) — ISBN 978-0-375-93393-6 (lib. bdg.)
[1. Fairy tales. 2. Dogs—Fiction.] I. Wu, Donald, ill. II. Title.
PZ8.B6375Do 2008 [E]—dc22 2007015229

Printed in the United States of America

10 9 8 7 6 5 4 3 2 1

First Edition

Dogerella

by Maribeth Boelts
illustrated by Donald Wu

Random House New York

Once upon a time,

there was a mean stepdog-mother

and two stepdog-sisters.

Dogerella was their servant.

"Dogerella! Fetch my chew toy!"

said one stepdog-sister.

"Dogerella! Scratch my fleas!"

said the other stepdog-sister.

"Dogerella! Fluff my tail!"

said the stepdog-mother.

At night, Dogerella curled up
by the fire.
She dreamed of a home
where she was loved.

Princess Bea lived in a palace.
For her fifth birthday,
she was given rubies.
For her sixth birthday,
she was given
rings and roses.

It would soon be
her seventh birthday.
Princess Bea did not want
rubies, rings, or roses.
She wanted a dog.

The queen fussed.

She told Princess Bea

that dogs were too silly.

They were too furry.

They went

to the bathroom outside!

"Can I go, too?"
asked Dogerella.
"Of course not,"
said her stepdog-mother.
She ordered Dogerella
to help them get ready.

Dogerella fluffed
their tangled tails.

She clipped
their yellow toenails.

She freshened
their doggy breath.

When they left for the ball,

Dogerella cried.

How she wished she could go!

Just then,
Dogerella's Fairy Dogmother
appeared.

She could make
Dogerella's wishes come true.
She waved her wand
over Dogerella's head.

"*Meow,*" said Dogerella.

She waved her wand again.

"Hee-haw," said Dogerella.

The Fairy Dogmother

put new batteries into her wand.

She waved it one last time.

Dogerella was turned back
into herself.
But she did have
a sparkly new collar.

There was no time to waste.
The Fairy Dogmother
clicked her paws
over a dog biscuit.

It turned into a mini-van.

Dogerella jumped in.

The mini-van raced to the palace.

At the palace,
Dogerella's heart pounded.

Some dogs wore crowns.
Some dogs had
broad chests and deep barks.
Some dogs had pink toenails
and extra-fluffy tails.
All the dogs looked their best.

Dogerella crawled
up the palace steps.
"Stop!" a guard shouted.
"A mutt like you
can't come to the ball!"

The guard put Dogerella

on a chain in the royal backyard.

Dogerella peeked
into a palace window.
She watched dogs
prance and dance
and do clever tricks.

But they also snapped

and snarled.

They stole

each other's royal treats, too.

The king patted
the best hunting dogs.
The queen petted
the prettiest dogs.

Princess Bea turned away.

She tried not to cry.

"I just want a dog

who is my *friend*,"

she said.

The king and queen

did not hear her.

But Dogerella did!

Her ears stood straight up.

She could be a friend

to Princess Bea!

Princess Bea left the ball.

She plopped down by the pond

in the royal backyard.

In the dark,

Dogerella wagged her tail.

She whimpered.

Princess Bea threw

the golden bone into the water.

Splash!

Dogerella pulled at the chain
around her neck.
She pulled so hard
her sparkly collar popped off!

She ran to the pond
and jumped in the water.

She paddled to the golden bone
and scooped it up.

"Here, dog!"

laughed Princess Bea.

Dogerella wagged her whole body

and dropped the bone.

"Good girl!" said Princess Bea.

Dogerella wiggled with joy.

Princess Bea

threw the bone again.

Dogerella brought it back.

Then she chased her tail.

She gave Princess Bea

her paw to shake.

Princess Bea picked up
the sparkly collar in the grass.
Whose was it?

Dogerella's mean stepdog-sisters

dashed from the palace.

They knocked into Princess Bea.

They barked and jumped.

Princess Bea tried the collar

on the first stepdog-sister.

It was too tight.

She tried it

on the second stepdog-sister.

It was too big.

She tried it on Dogerella.

It fit just right!

Princess Bea gave Dogerella
a hug.

Dogerella licked her cheek.

In the palace,

Princess Bea told everyone

the good news.

Dogerella would get

the golden bone.

She would be the royal pet.

The other dogs

stomped their paws.

They growled and howled.

They nipped and yipped.

"The ball is over,"

said Princess Bea.

But none of the dogs would leave.

"What will we do?"

asked Princess Bea.

Suddenly,

the Fairy Dogmother came to help.

She waved her wand.

A carriage
filled with cats appeared.
Dogs chased cats
out of the palace
and into the woods.

"That's much better,"
said Princess Bea.
"Now we can live
happily ever after . . .
together!"

"*Woof!*" said Dogerella.